Bang

Bang

Norah McClintock

orca soundings

Orca Book Publishers

Library and Archives Canada Cataloguing in Publication

McClintock, Norah
Bang / written by Norah McClintock.
(Orca soundings)
ISBN 978-1-55143-656-2 (bound)
ISBN 978-1-55143-654-8 (pbk.)
I. Title.
PS8575.C62B35 2007 jC813'.54 C2006-907056-3

Summary: A robbery goes terribly wrong, and Quentin
finds he is left taking the blame.

First published in the United States, 2007
Library of Congress Control Number: 2006940639

Orca Book Publishers gratefully acknowledges the support for its
publishing programs provided by the following agencies: the Government
of Canada through the Book Publishing Industry Development Program
and the Canada Council for the Arts, and the Province of British Columbia
through the BC Arts Council and the Book Publishing Tax Credit.

Cover design: Doug McCaffry
Cover photography: Getty Images

Orca Book Publishers   Orca Book Publishers
PO Box 5626, Station B   PO Box 468
Victoria, BC Canada   Custer, WA USA
V8R 6S4   98240-0468

www.orcabook.com
Printed and bound in Canada.
Printed on 100% PCW recycled paper.
010 09 08 07 • 5 4 3 2 1

To Tiny, Skinny and Halftrack.

Chapter One

The way the day starts: Sweet. Perfect. Like a cool breeze on a hot day. Mainly because of Leah. She answers the door when I ring the bell and stays to talk until JD comes down.

And then, before we take off on our bikes, she says, "Wait."

She runs inside and gets her camera. "It's brand-new," she says. "It's digital. I saved up for it."

She takes our picture—JD and me with our bikes. Then she says, "Hey, JD, take my picture with Q." So JD does.

I ask her to make me a copy of it. If she does, I'll put it up on my wall, right over my bed. These days, Leah is most of the reason I spend as much time with JD as I do. I'm trying to work up the nerve to ask her out.

The way the day ends: Like a tornado, sucking my whole life up and spraying out the pieces all over town so I'll never be able to put it back together again.

The first thing we do when we get back to JD's house is strip off all our clothes, right down to our shorts. JD wants those too, but I say no. There's no way I'm going to stand there in his kitchen buck naked.

He sends me up to his room to grab some clothes. When I come back down, JD has stuffed all our clothes into the washing machine, which is in a sort of closet off the kitchen. He pours in a ton of liquid detergent, turns on the water and punches

"On." I'm pulling on a clean T-shirt of his when Leah walks in.

She looks at me, then at JD, and says, "What are you guys up to?"

"We were riding our bikes in the ravine," JD says. "Q had this idea we could jump the stream." He gives me a look. "I should have known."

Q is me. My name is Quentin, Q to my friends.

Leah shakes her head, like *of course* I would suggest something that dumb. *Of course* JD would want to give it a try. *Of course* that would explain why she's just caught me changing into JD's clothes in the middle of the kitchen.

I stare at JD, trying not to let my face show what I'm thinking, which is: This guy is good. He can lie with the best of them. No, he can lie *better* than most of them.

Leah says, "Well, I hope you didn't total your bike, JD, because if you did, Dad's going to freak."

I freeze. Our bikes. Geez, they're in JD's garage, but there's nothing about them that would give people the idea that we tried to jump a stream with them, let alone that we ended up *in* a stream. They aren't wet. They aren't muddy. Nothing like that.

"Don't sweat it," JD tells his sister.

Even now I can't help noticing for the millionth time how pretty she is. I wonder, How come I only started noticing recently? I've known JD since kindergarten, which means I've known Leah that long too. But for most of the time I've known her, she was like flowery wallpaper, always in the background, always kind of annoying.

Not anymore. Now I can hardly take my eyes off her. She has thick brown hair and dark brown eyes that are the color of coffee, just like JD's. She's tall, like JD, and slender, and she makes my heart pound and my mouth go dry. Her lips are pink and soft looking and, boy, you don't need much imagination to know how it would feel to kiss them. That's been on my mind a lot—that and how JD would take it if I all of a sudden tell him I have a thing for his sister. Now, I think, I'll never get the chance. Not after what we just did.

"We're going out to the garage right now," JD says. "We're going to clean everything up before Dad gets home. Our bikes will be as good as new. He'll never know."

He flashes her a smile. She shakes her head again, but I can read in her eyes how much she loves him. They're twins. They have this bond. He says it's weird having a twin. He says when they were little, they used to finish each other's sentences. He says half the time he's positive she can tell what he's thinking. I look at Leah now and wonder what she knows. I look at JD too. He's grinning at her. I bet he's confident that he's snowing her. I hope he's right.

"Don't make a mess out there while you're cleaning up," Leah says. Boy, does she ever know JD. "You know how Dad is."

We go from the kitchen to the garage. Our bikes are dry. There's no mud on them, nothing at all on them that I can see. But JD fills a bucket with soapy water anyway and hands me a sponge. We set to work washing down our bikes. We rinse them. JD fills another bucket with soapy water. We wash them again and rinse them again. Altogether we soap and rinse three times before JD is satisfied. He looks at me and says, "It's going to be okay. I already told you. Nobody saw. Nobody knows."

He's forgetting one thing. *I* saw. *I* know.

Chapter Two

The guy died. I'm not surprised. Also, I'm relieved. I can't believe I feel that way, but I do. I'm actually relieved because if he's dead, that means he can't say anything.

I'm staring at the TV. The news is over. The guy's death was the last item and now the weather guy is doing his thing. In the kitchen, the phone rings. A moment later, my mother appears and hands me the cordless. She says, "It's JD."

The first words out of JD's mouth are "You should get a cell phone."

Right. "You gonna pay for it?" I say.

As usual, he doesn't answer. Instead he says, "You heard, right? It's like I told you, we have nothing to worry about."

I realize he's talking about the dead guy. He must have seen the news too.

"You're okay, right, Q?" he says. "You're cool, right?"

"Yeah," I say. I'm thinking, They said the guy is dead. But they didn't say exactly *when* he died. Was it before the paramedics arrived? I can't believe I'm thinking it, but I am—it would be best if he died before the paramedics showed up. But what if he didn't? What if he was alive long enough to talk to them? What would he have told them? What *could* he have told them?

"Hey, Q, you haven't talked to anyone, have you?" JD says.

"No," I say. But JD isn't satisfied.

"Why don't you come over here?" he says. "Spend the night."

"It's all good," I insist. "Really."

JD is...*was*...my best friend. We've slept over at each other's places since kindergarten. Boy, the things we've done. But tonight there's no way I want to go to his house. No way I want to be anywhere near him.

"I'll see you tomorrow," I say.

"I'll pick you up," he says, meaning he'll swing by my house on the way to school. "First thing," he says.

At first I can't sleep. I keep seeing it and hearing it and even tasting it. How can you sleep when you've seen a thing like that? The next thing I know, my mother is hammering on my door, telling me to get up or I'm going to be late. Telling me my lunch is in the fridge. Telling me she's leaving for work now and if I'm late and I get a detention—*again*—and have to be late for my after-school job and get fired and have no money for the stuff I like to waste money on, that's not going to be her problem. In other words, telling me the same thing she tells me every morning before she rushes off to work herself. I yell through the door that I'm awake and I'm getting up. What I'm thinking is, I can't believe I slept. I feel as guilty about that as I do about what happened.

Five minutes later, I'm dressed and shoveling some Cap'n Crunch into my mouth. I can't believe I can eat after what happened. I hear footsteps out in the hall and someone rings the bell. I peer through the peephole. It's JD. The cereal starts to roll around in my stomach like it doesn't want to be there anymore, like it wants to get out, *now*.

"Hey, Q," JD calls through the door. "Open up."

I unlock the door and swing it open. JD looks as calm and cool as he always does. It's obvious he's slept well. It's obvious he doesn't have a care in the world. He looks me over and says, "The main thing is you have to relax. If you relax, if you act normal, it's gonna be okay. No one saw anything. We're in the clear."

Act normal? The guy died, and JD wants me to act normal? I think he must be crazy. But you know what? Even though the guy died, I remember to take the brown paper bag containing my lunch out of the fridge and put it in my backpack. I remember to grab my geography homework off the end of the dinette table. I put it in my backpack too. And just as I'm going out the door, I remember that even though school started only two weeks ago, my history teacher has already planned a field trip to the museum. This is the last day to hand in the permission slip. So I go back into the kitchen and get it off the fridge door where my mother stuck it after she signed it. I lock up after myself. We take the stairs instead of the elevator because at this time of the morning, with everyone headed off to school or work, the elevator takes forever.

At school I'm kind of surprised to find that no one is talking about the only thing that's on my mind. I say that to JD when we're at the far end of the football field at lunchtime. I say, "You don't think it's weird that no one's even mentioned it?"

He looks out across the field and says, "Why would they? I bet you no one here even heard of the guy. Stuff happens to people all the time and no one notices, not unless they know the person it happened to."

That's when I start wondering about the dead guy. Someone must have known him. Maybe a lot of someones. And *they're* probably talking about him. They're probably wondering who did it and why. Some of them are probably crying. Was he married? Did he have kids? Maybe he was looking after his old granny. Or maybe his mother is sick and he was looking after her and now there's no one to take his place. I think about all that and I start to shake.

JD says, "What's the matter with you?" like he can't even begin to imagine. Then he says, "You better smile right now because here comes Leah."

And there she is, swinging along toward us, wearing a T-shirt and a short skirt.

Her long legs are still tanned from the summer.

"JD," she says, smiling at him, "what are you doing way over here? Up to no good, I bet." If she only knew.

"Hey, Leah," I manage to say, practically choking on the words because my mouth is so dry.

"What's up?" JD says as smooth as ever.

"I had to pay Melissa back the money I borrowed from her last week, and now I'm broke. Can you lend me some money? I want to stop by the mall on the way home. They're having a sale."

JD digs in his pocket and brings out his wallet. He's got a few twenties in there, a few tens, and some fives. He always has money on him, and it's always more than I make in a week. JD doesn't have a job, though. He doesn't need one. He has both a father and a mother. They both work, and they both make good money. JD is always telling me, "My parents say we have plenty of time to look for work after high school. They say in the meantime we should concentrate on school and have a good time. They say that, after high school, things get more serious."

We still have another year after this one. If you ask me, things are already as serious as they're ever going to get.

Chapter Three

I'm restocking the soup aisle in the grocery store where I work after school, four to seven, five days a week. I stack the cans twelve deep, two high, two across—forty-eight cans of cream of tomato, forty-eight cans of cream of mushroom, forty-eight cans of chicken noodle, and so on and so on. There's maybe fifty or sixty different kinds of canned soup. My job right now is to make sure that whichever one a customer wants, it's there. And if they want two or three cans, it's my job to make sure they're available.

I'm restocking the soup aisle, but I'm thinking back to how it started. I'm asking myself, Why did I do something so stupid? Answer: Because I wasn't thinking straight. I can see it like it's happening right in front of me. It goes like this: JD and I have just smoked up, I admit it, and now we're horsing around. It's no big deal. There's no one else in the park. No one that I can see anyway. The playground is empty and we're a little high. We think it would be fun to go on the swings and see how much higher we can get, if you know what I mean. So that's what we do. We get on and we pump and pump until we are flying. Yeah, I know, we probably look stupid, a couple of sixteen-year-old guys flying on a pair of swings. But I've seen people a lot older than me on those swings sometimes. I've seen girls who are maybe seventeen or eighteen playing on those swings. I've seen moms being pushed by their husbands. And anyway, like I said, the park is empty.

A couple of little kids come up the path that runs diagonally through the park. A little boy and a little girl. They look maybe seven or eight years old. They must live nearby because there's no adult with them. It's just the two of them. They go down the slide a few times each. Then they come over to the swings. They just stand there, watching, until finally JD says, "Scram!"

The two kids look at each other. The little boy says, "We want a turn on the swings."

JD says, "Forget it. These are *our* swings."

The little girl looks like she's going to cry. She whispers something to the boy, but I can't hear what it is.

"Get out of here," JD says, his voice deeper than usual. "Otherwise I'll have to come over there and grab you and lock you up in my cave." He laughs a wicked-troll laugh, all evil and scary.

The little girl's eyes get big and watery. She tugs on the little boy's arm. They run back down the path. JD laughs. I think, Geez, next thing you know, their father is going to show up and he's going to be pissed at us.

Then this man appears out of nowhere. He stops right in front of us, just out of range of the swings, his arms folded over his chest. He looks like a school principal, his face stern and disapproving.

JD slows down enough so he can say to the guy, "Why don't you take a picture? It'll last longer." And then, JD being JD, he starts to laugh at what a smart remark he's just made.

"Why don't *you* act your age?" the man says. "Those swings are for little kids to play on, not for teenagers who have been smoking up."

That makes me stop pumping. The man must have smelled us. Maybe he has been watching us for a while. Maybe he saw us pass the joint back and forth down by the big tree over on one side of the park.

"Come on," I say to JD. I drag my feet through the sand under the swing to slow myself down. "Let's get out of here."

But JD is pumping his legs again.

"There aren't any little kids around," he says. He swears at the man and tells him to mind his own business.

The man's stern face gets even sterner.

"You talk like that," the man says, "it only shows how ignorant you are and what a poor vocabulary you have."

That does it. JD jumps off the swing when it's still pretty high. He lands right in front of the man.

"What's your problem?" he says. "You got nothing better to do than harass people who are using a *public* park?"

"You're right," the man says. "It is a public park. Which means little children have a right to play here without some ignorant fool like you bullying them."

I get off my swing and go over to JD. "Come on," I say. "Let's get out of here. We don't need any trouble."

"I see your friend has more brains than you," the man says to JD. "Because if you don't go, I *will* call the police, and I *will* report you for marijuana use.

JD just laughs. "Get real," he says. "The cops aren't arresting anyone for smoking anymore." It's true. They're still busting people for growing it and selling it, but they're not making arrests for just smoking it. JD explained it to me one time. It has something to do with a Supreme Court case that happened, and now the government is taking another look at the law. While it does, the cops have stopped arresting people for simple possession.

"If I call the cops, they'll take your names and they'll take your pot," the man says. That's true too. If the cops catch you, they write everything down with the idea that as soon as the law is clarified, they can charge you. In the meantime, you're out your weed.

JD swears again. Then he says what I've been saying the whole time: "Let's get out of here." He swaggers up the path ahead of me to the swimming pool and disappears behind the building where the change rooms are.

I'm right behind him until the guy says

to me, "You should think about your life and what you're doing with it. When it's all over, what do you want people to say about you? There was a guy who really accomplished something? Or there was a guy who was just taking up space?"

I stare at him. He stares right back at me. Then he turns away. What a jerk, I think. He doesn't even know me and he's coming on all heavy with me. I raise my hand and point at him. I make like I'm pulling the trigger of a gun. Bang, mister, I say to myself. Now who's taking up space?

I hurry up the path to catch JD. I figure that's the end of that. And it is. For one day.

Chapter Four

I keep stacking and arranging soup cans in the supermarket while I remember what happened the next day. I can see it like I'm watching a movie.

It goes like this: The next day, I ride over to JD's house on my bike to get him. We're going to hang around, you know, take it easy on a September Sunday. School has just started, and so far we don't have much homework. So why not make the most of it, especially when it's nice and cool—I'm wearing a long-sleeved shirt, and JD is wearing a big, floppy, long-sleeved T-shirt that hangs down almost to his knees—but sunny and bright? Oh yeah, and I'm also hoping to catch a glimpse of Leah. I do. She takes our picture. I'm hoping maybe she'll come out with us. She doesn't. She's going somewhere with one of her girlfriends.

We leave JD's house, ride our bikes a couple of blocks, duck down an alley behind a medical building that's closed, and smoke up. Then we argue about what to do. I want to head downtown, maybe hang out at an arcade for a while. JD wants to go to the beach, where it's nice and relaxed. Where he says there will be girls sitting in the sun, working at keeping the color in their faces. He says he saw some girls down there the other day. Pretty girls. He says he should try to meet them. He's really into the idea. Me, I can't imagine being interested in anyone except Leah. But of course we end up at the beach. We lock up our bikes. We smoke up again and goof around over by the tennis courts, where three girls are sitting under a tree, talking and giggling. JD tells me those are the girls. He says he likes one of them, a redhead with green eyes.

"And I bet you're interested in the blond," he says to me. "The one with the brown hair, she's a dog, huh?"

I want to tell him, no, the only girl I'm interested in is Leah, but I don't have the nerve. I've seen how JD reacts to other guys who come on to Leah—he doesn't like it. I don't know how he'd react if I turned into one of those guys. So I just shrug and hope that's the end of it.

It isn't.

JD goes over to the girls. Of course he expects me to go with him. Only one of the girls, the one with the brown hair who JD thinks is ugly, pays any attention to us at first. She isn't the best-looking girl in the world, but up close she's not that bad looking either. Plus she has amazingly large, pale blue eyes. JD doesn't even glance at her. He's trying hard to get the redhead to talk to him.

"You can forget about her," the girl with the brown hair says. "She's got a boyfriend."

"Yeah?" JD says. "Does her boyfriend drive a Jag?" He's looking at the redhead when he says it.

I look at him like he's crazy. We came here on our bikes. JD doesn't have a car, let alone a Jag. He only has his learner's license, which means he can't even drive unless there's a seriously sober licensed driver sitting right up front with him. Still, the question gets him what he wants. The redhead turns to look at him.

"You telling me you do?" she says. She has a stuck-up voice, like she's the queen of something.

JD grins at her but doesn't answer the question.

"You should tell your friend to back off," the girl with the brown hair says to me. "Her boyfriend's the jealous type. And he's tough, if you know what I mean."

JD is still grinning.

"Tough?" he says. He hasn't taken his eyes off the redhead. "How tough is he? Is he as tough as this?"

I'm standing a little behind him when he says this, mostly because I want to be out of there. I don't want to talk to the stuck-up redhead with a tough jealous boyfriend. I don't want to try to get her icy blond friend to say a word. And I am one hundred percent not interested in the girl with the brown hair. JD reaches behind him, up under his big T-shirt. Because of where I'm standing, I see what he's doing. He's getting ready to pull something out from underneath. I do a major double-take when I see what it is. I tell myself it can't be real. But you never know with JD. So I grab the arm that's reaching behind him and pull him away from the girls. "Are you crazy?" I say.

"What?" he says. He is annoyed with me, like I've just ruined his big chance with the redhead.

I hear a car horn honk up at the road. The three girls turn. The redhead waves

I still can't believe what I've seen.

"You got a gun so you could impress a girl?" I say. "Geez, she wouldn't even talk to you."

JD keeps right on smiling. "Maybe I lost the battle," he says, "but I'm going to win the war."

Right.

to someone in a black Mustang with tinted windows.

"Her boyfriend," the girl with the brown hair says. The three of them waggle their butts as they walk toward the car. JD stares at the redhead and shakes his head.

"Is that for real?" I ask him.

"Is what for real?"

"You know," I say. I drop my voice to a whisper. "That gun you have stuck in the back of your pants."

JD smiles at me. "Yeah, it's for real."

I have a million questions: Where did you get it? Why did you get it? Why are you carrying it around like that? Why would you want to show it to a bunch of girls? What if they decided to call the cops? There's no way that gun is legal.

JD says, "Relax. That redhead, she would never call the cops."

"How do you know that?" I say.

"I know who she is. I know who her boyfriend is. She's one of those girls who likes guys with muscle cars and tinted windows, probably with the bass cranked up."

Chapter Five

I'm in the grocery store, stacking soup cans, and I'm thinking, Best friend or not, I should never have hooked up with JD again.

He got into some trouble last year. JD is like that, always into something. He always has some weed, and everyone knows you can buy it off him. But this last time, JD really laid into a guy. He says it was because of what the guy said about Leah. But he hurt the guy pretty bad. The cops got involved. In the end, JD's father got him off by agreeing to send JD to a special camp over the summer. JD says it was like a prison camp. The counselors yell at you all day. You have to get up at six in the morning, and you're always doing something—hiking for days at a time, going on long canoe trips, always something physical so that you collapse at the end of the day. And it doesn't matter what the weather is, either. If you go on a weeklong hike and it rains every day, too bad for you.

When JD got back, he was tanned and a lot stronger than he used to be. He acts differently now too, but probably not in the way the camp hoped he would. He has more confidence. He knows more people. He's told me about some of the guys he met at the camp. Boy, I bet he hasn't told his dad about those guys. Some of them sound scary. I shouldn't have hooked up with him again.

But he called me when he got back.

And I was hoping to get with Leah, who

was also away at camp all summer, but not the same kind of camp. She had a job as a counselor at a kids' camp up in cottage country.

So when he called and asked me to come over so we could catch up, I said, "Sure." But I should have said no. I should have stayed away from him. Then it never would have happened.

The worst thing is, it was my fault.

What happened: After the girls pile into the black Mustang with the tinted windows, JD and I get on our bikes and ride through the park. I can tell he's antsy, probably because he didn't get what he wanted. He didn't get the redhead. I try to get his mind off the girl. I say we should get something to eat. He's not interested. We keep riding until finally we're out of the park that runs along the beach. We turn and ride north and find ourselves close to another park that's more or less in our neighborhood. This is the park with the swings we were on the day before. I'm really hungry now.

Partly it's because of all the weed and partly it's because by now it's three o'clock in the afternoon. We've been riding all day. The only thing in my stomach is a bowl of cold cereal, and it's probably not there anymore because I ate it hours ago.

We're riding along and I just happen to glance down an alley. And I just happen to see one of those canteen vans. You know, the ones that you see on the street down by city hall. The ones that show up at construction sites. You can buy coffee and pop, cookies and donuts, sandwiches, burgers, hot dogs, fries. All that kind of stuff. So there's one sitting in the alley. The rear door is open and I can see inside. My eye goes right to a rack filled with bags of potato chips. Suddenly there's nothing in the world I want more than a bag of potato chips. Maybe two bags.

I detour into the alley and lean my bike up against a brick wall. Behind me I hear JD say, "Now what?"

I check out the alley. No one is around. None of the buildings have windows that look down into the alley. No one can see me.

I duck into the van and grab a couple of bags of potato chips. Then I see a freezer. Inside are some ice-cream bars and ice-cream sandwiches. I grab a handful of those.

"As long as you're in there," JD says, "you see anything to drink?"

I toss the chips and the ice-cream bars to him and open a cooler to get some pop. I'm jumping down out of the van with it when a door opens and a man steps into the alley. He's wearing a shirt with the same logo on it that's on the van, so I know the canteen van is his. I start to run, but he's fast and he grabs me. He has a grip of iron. He isn't about to let me go. Then I realize who it is. It's the same guy who gave us a hard time in the park the day before. The guy who threatened to call the cops on us. At first I want to laugh. Mr. Accomplishment gives me a lecture about taking up space and it turns out his big accomplishment is running a canteen van. Like one of those girl country singers says, That don't impress me much.

I get over wanting to laugh when I try to break free of the guy. He isn't big but, boy, is he strong. He's got a real good hold on me, and now he's reaching for JD. He says, "I knew you two were trouble the first time I laid eyes on you. I'm making a citizen's arrest."

I remember thinking, Boy, this guy is nuts. Everyone knows it's stupid to make a citizen's arrest. Anything could happen. In the first place, there are two of us and only one of him—not that this is slowing him down. In the second place, it would be his word against ours and, like I said, there are two of us. Except that JD has already been in trouble before and it could go hard on him. I'm thinking that exact thought when it happens.

JD dodges the guy. I try to break free, but the guy holds tight.

I see JD back up in the alley. I think, Great, he's going to take off and leave me in the guy's clutches. The guy even seems ready to let JD go because he grabs me with both hands now. He looks determined. There's no way he's going to let me go.

Then JD says, "Hey, mister?"

The guy and I both turn our heads to look at him.

JD hasn't taken off. He's come back and he's just standing there, close enough that the guy could grab him if he wanted to. He's looking at the guy. I see him reach behind with one hand. I start to shake my head, but JD pulls out the gun and points it at the guy. The guy's eyes bulge when he sees it. Then his mouth turns up into a grin, the same kind of superior I-know-everything-and-you-know-nothing grin that you'd expect from a vice-principal.

"What are you going to do?" he says to JD. "Shoot me?"

JD's face changes. It gets hard. He pulls the trigger.

Chapter Six

I'm standing in the alley, frozen and burning up all at the same time. The noise from the gun is deafening. I can't understand why there aren't a hundred people running into the alley to see what happened.

But there aren't.

The guy is on the ground. Blood is pooling around him. I can't tell if he's breathing or not.

I'm just standing there, looking at JD.
I can't believe he shot the guy. I can't
believe he did it when the guy was still
holding on to me. I think, What if he
missed the guy and hit me? Did he even
think about that?

Then, I don't even know how, we're
on our bikes and we're riding down the
alley. My first thought is to get out of
the alley the same way we came in. But
JD grabs my arm and heads off in the
other direction. I follow him. I'm totally
uncoordinated. It's like I've just got my
training wheels off and I'm not sure of
my balance. But I follow him, pedaling
fast. The alley joins with another alley,
so we turn and ride down there. JD slows
down when we get close to the end of it.
He makes me slow down too. It's torture
because all I want is to get out of there
as fast as possible. But I do what JD is
doing. I take it easy. We ride casually
out of the alley, JD in the lead. We ride
leisurely down one block, then another.
My heart is pounding the whole time. My

legs are itching to go faster, go faster. We make another turn and JD really powers on the speed.

Finally we get to JD's house, where we put our bikes in the garage. We go into the house and JD starts pulling off his clothes. At first I think he's crazy. Then he points to my shirt. I look down. There's blood all over it. There's some other stuff on it too, but I don't know what it is and I don't want to think about it.

"We've got to wash these," JD says. "We've got to wash everything. You've seen those shows on TV. They can find stuff that we can't even see."

They can find stuff? He means the cops can find stuff. I start to shake all over.

"Relax," JD says. "No one saw anything. And I didn't see anyone. Just give me your clothes."

When I don't move, JD comes over and starts to unbutton the denim shirt I'm wearing, like I'm a little kid and he's my mother. I jerk away from him, mad that he's touching me. Mad that there's blood on my shirt. Mad that he had that stupid gun sticking in the back of his pants.

"You have to give me your clothes, Q," he says. He's already peeled off everything, and I mean everything. There is a stack of clean bath towels sitting on top of the dryer. He wraps one around his waist. "Come on," he said. "We have to wash everything *now*."

I take everything off except my underwear. JD hands me a towel. He says, "Go up to my room and find us some clothes. I'll start the washing machine."

So I do. And while I'm getting dressed, Leah shows up. Then JD and I go into the garage and wash our bikes, just in case. And while we're doing that, JD says, "If I get caught, they'll lock me up. They'll probably want to try me as an adult and try to get me an adult sentence. You too, Q. You were robbing the guy when it happened. They go hard when it's a robbery where someone gets killed."

We stand there for a few minutes looking at each other. We're probably both wondering the same thing: How did a day that started off okay go so wrong?

And now here it is, the day after the guy died. I'm stocking the soup aisle in the grocery store after school, thinking, Now what?

I make a lot of mistakes. I mix the tomato-and-rice soup in with the cream of tomato. I put the celery soup with the mushroom soup because, on the label, the pictures of the bowls of celery soup and the bowls of mushroom soup look the same. I put chicken noodle with chicken and rice. It wouldn't be such a big deal except the manager comes by and looks at what I'm doing. Nobody likes him. People are quitting all the time, if they're not getting fired. The main reason people quit is that it's hard to work for someone like him. He's the kind of guy who likes the shelves fully stocked all the time, no excuses, and the products to be straight and neat. If that means you have to work through your break or put in a little (free) time after your shift, then that's what he expects. He looks at my work and tells me, "Do it again. And do it right this time." He also says, "If I have to tell you a second time to do it again, you won't be working here anymore." See what I mean?

When I finally get off, half an hour later than I should because of the do-over, JD is waiting for me out on the sidewalk. I get that frozen-burning up feeling again.

"Geez, relax, will you?" JD says. He puts an arm around my shoulder to steer me away from the store. "You look like you're going to jump out of your skin." Once we're away from the store, he lets go of me.

"What's wrong?" I say. "What happened?"

He gives me a look. "Nothing happened. Nothing's going to happen."

"Then why are you here?"

He laughs. "I'm glad to see you too, Q," he says.

"I'm serious, JD. What are you doing here?"

"I just want to make sure you're okay," he says. "You looked so freaked out at school. You need to stay calm, Q. You can't panic. If you panic, something bad will happen. If you stay calm, everything will be fine. Okay?"

"Did you hear anything? Was there anything on the news?"

"Nothing," JD says. "The guy was just a guy. He wasn't anything special. No one's going to make a big fuss over him."

"Yeah, but the cops are going to want to find out who did it."

"Sure they are," JD says. How can he be so cool about this? "But what are they going to find? No one saw anything, remember?"

But I'm thinking, Just because we didn't see anyone, that doesn't mean no one saw us.

It turns out I'm right.

Chapter Seven

How I find out I'm right is this: I'm at home alone. My mom is on the evening shift. She works in the kitchen at one of those chain restaurants. I don't have a father. Well, I do, somewhere. But he left my mom when I was two years old and has never been back in touch. I don't remember him.

So I'm at home with a plate of warmed-up macaroni casserole on my lap that I haven't even touched, and I'm watching the local news. I'm just about thinking that JD is right, maybe the cops are on the case but no one else is, when up pops a picture of the guy that died. It hangs there, a little behind and just to the right of the guy who's reading the news. The guy reading says that the police are looking for a male between the ages of sixteen and twenty-one who was seen in the vicinity of the shooting. They give this description of the male suspect: medium build, sandy-colored hair, wearing blue jeans and a blue shirt. I feel like I'm going to throw up, even though I haven't eaten a bite since breakfast. The announcer says if anyone has any information, they should call the police or Crime Stoppers.

I'm still staring at the TV half an hour later when someone hammers on the apartment door. The warmed-up macaroni casserole is cold. I'm waiting for a loud voice to say, "Police. Open up."

Instead what I hear is "Hey, Q, it's me."

JD.

I want him to go away. I don't want to see him ever again.

He says, "I know you're in there. I can hear the TV."

I get up and shut off the TV. I put the plate of cold macaroni casserole in the kitchen. I open the apartment door.

"I figured maybe you could use some company," JD says. He inspects me. "You saw the news, right?"

"Yes," I say, and my voice doesn't sound right. It's high, like a girl's. "I saw it. Did you? Did you hear—"

JD puts a finger to his lips to silence me. He pushes me inside the apartment. Before he comes in, he looks up and down the hall. Then he closes the door behind him and moves me along into the living room.

"You really have to calm down," he says. It's practically the only thing he says to me anymore. "You keep panicking and yelling like that, you might as well turn yourself in."

"Turn *myself* in?" I say. "I'm not the one who shot the guy."

JD's voice is soft and low. "What I mean is, you keep yelling like that, maybe one of your neighbors will get the wrong idea."

"But you heard what they said on the news. They're looking for a guy who looks just like me."

JD shakes his head. "They're looking for a medium-build guy with sandy hair who was wearing jeans and a blue shirt. Do you have any idea how many people in a city this size fit that description?"

"But what if whoever saw that much got a good look at me? What if he can identify me?"

"If he could identify you," JD says, "the cops would be here already and they wouldn't have to put that description out to the media."

That makes sense. Then I remember something. "What about my clothes? Are they still in your dryer?"

JD shakes his head again. "I took care of them."

"What do you mean?"

"Those CSI guys on TV, they can find all kinds of things you'd never even know were there. So I took our clothes and I burned them."

This surprises me and, to be honest, scares me a little. It makes me think that maybe JD isn't as calm as he looks. Maybe he's worried too.

"When did you do that?" I say.

"This afternoon, after school."

"Where?" I say.

"You don't have to worry about that," JD says. "Just some place out of the way."

"Did anyone see you?"

"No."

"You sure?"

"Yeah, I'm sure. And I made sure that the fire burned everything. Then I shoveled up all the ashes and buried them in another place away from where I made the fire. Nobody's ever going to find those clothes, believe me."

I start to relax.

"They didn't even mention the bikes," JD says. "They're looking for a guy who was on foot. For all we know, whoever the police have as a witness didn't even see you. Maybe they saw some other sandy-haired guy in jeans nearby. Seriously, Q, take a look around our school sometime. See how many people fit that general description."

I decide he's right. We sit down on the couch and JD reaches for the remote. He turns on the TV and we watch a couple of shows together. Then we go into the bathroom and smoke up. By the time he leaves at midnight, I am one hundred percent relaxed. I shove the macaroni casserole into the microwave, nuke it and eat the whole thing. Right afterward, I'm so tired I can't keep my eyes open. I stagger into bed with my clothes still on and fall asleep. The last thought I have is, It's going to be okay.

It isn't.

Chapter Eight

My mother is up early the next morning, which surprises me. Usually when she works late, she sleeps late.

"I have a doctor's appointment," she says, looking through from the kitchen at the TV in the living room. She's watching one of those breakfast television shows, the ones that give you news and weather, but also give you cooking tips, decorating tips and interviews with celebrities.

"A doctor's appointment?" I say. I wonder if I should be worried.

My mother tells me right away, "It's nothing. Just a routine checkup." She drinks down the last of her coffee and puts the mug in the sink. She is wiping her hands on a clean dishtowel when there's a newsbreak. A reporter is standing outside a police station. There's a plainclothes cop with him who turns out to be a homicide detective. He tells the reporter that the person they're looking for in relation to the shooting in an alley was probably riding a bicycle.

"Isn't that terrible," my mother says. She looks right at me. "I heard it was a kid who did it. Someone close to your age. Why do you suppose a kid would shoot someone like that?"

I don't answer, which is okay. She isn't really expecting an answer. I keep looking at the TV. The reporter asks about violent crime in the city and talks about all the people who have been shot lately. He asks the homicide detective why there is so much gun crime. My mother grabs her purse and kisses me on the cheek.

"I'm off at nine tonight. I'll leave supper for you," she says.

Someone knocks at the door and I hear my mother greet JD. She leaves and he comes in, backpack over one shoulder, just as the police show what they call a composite sketch of the suspect. I stare at it and really relax for the first time since it happened. If you ask me, the guy in the sketch doesn't look anything like me. Grinning, I glance at JD.

"You were right," I say. "Whoever they have as a witness didn't see two guys, just one. For sure he didn't see me—or you. Either that or they have a police artist who flunked out of art school."

JD stares at me. He has a funny expression on his face.

"Are you okay?" I say.

He nods. "Can I use your bathroom?"

While he's in there, I pour myself a big bowl of cereal and eat the whole thing. I make myself a peanut butter and honey sandwich and eat that, washing it down with a glass of milk. I feel great. The face on that drawing doesn't look like me at all. I feel like dancing. If Leah was here, I'd grab her and swing her around. Who knows, maybe I'd even kiss her.

JD comes into the kitchen and says, "We better get a move on."

"No problem," I say.

I'm practically walking on air all the way to school. Sure, I'm sorry about the guy who got killed. But I wasn't the one carrying the gun. I didn't do anything. Only now I don't have to try to explain that to the police. I don't have to explain anything to anybody. I don't have to rat out JD, which I have the feeling he wouldn't take very well, if you know what I mean. All I have to do is try to forget about the whole thing.

The morning goes like normal—attendance, announcements, math, computers, French. In other words, boring, boring, boring, computer games, boring. Except that Leah is in my French class. On her way to her desk, she hands me an envelope.

"What is it?" I say.

"Open it," she says.

I do and find a picture of JD and me with our bikes. It's the picture Leah took Sunday morning. It's the last thing I want to be reminded of. But she's standing there waiting for my reaction, so I tell her, It's great, thanks, Leah.

She frowns. "What's the matter? Don't you like it?"

"Sure, I do," I say. Then I tell her the truth. "I was hoping it would be the picture JD took. The one of you and me."

Her cheeks turn pink. "Really?"

"Yeah, really."

She looks at me in a way she's never done before, and all of a sudden I wish we weren't in French class. I wish we were somewhere alone together.

After she takes her place, I fold the picture of JD and me and tuck it into my wallet.

Just before French class ends, there's

an announcement to the whole school over the PA system—special assembly after lunch. Students whose last names start with the letters A to L report to the auditorium at one o'clock. Students whose last names start with M to Z report at one thirty. The vice-principal who makes the announcement doesn't say what the special assembly is all about.

JD and I are both M-Z, so we report to the auditorium from English class (the only class we're in together) at one thirty. Kids from the one o'clock assembly are making their way back to class. JD snags one of them, a kid he knows, and asks him what the assembly is about.

"Some guy who got shot," the kid says. "The cops think maybe it was a kid from this school that did it."

There it is again—that freezing hot feeling. Plus I feel like I want to throw up.

JD gives me a little push to get me moving down the hall toward the auditorium. We take a seat in the back. The vice-principal is on the stage telling everyone, Settle down, come on, people, we don't have all day. When it's finally quiet, he introduces a man in a sharp-looking suit. I recognize him. He's the homicide cop that was on the breakfast television show. He tells us his name—Detective Brian Tanner. He says he is working on the murder of Richard Braithwaite, who was shot in an alley only a few blocks from where we are sitting right now. He says Mr. Braithwaite—the whole rest of the time he talks about him, he calls him mister—came to this country from Trinidad with not much more than a dime in his pocket. He says Mr. Braithwaite worked hard at a lot of different jobs before he was able to buy himself a truck, and that he was well-known on construction sites for his food—especially Caribbean food—and for his sense of humor. I glance at JD. It's news to us that the guy even had a sense of humor.

The homicide cop tells us that Mr. Braithwaite coached soccer for a local league. He also volunteered at a breakfast club at one of the elementary schools in the neighborhood, and he spent every Sunday afternoon at a nursing home, playing piano for the old people. Oh yeah, he was also a volunteer dog walker for the humane society. The guy was a real saint. The homicide cop tells us the guy's funeral was that morning and the church was packed to overflowing with kids, their parents, teachers and old people. Everybody loved Mr. Braithwaite.

Then the cop tells us that he needs help if the police are going to catch whoever shot Mr. Braithwaite. He says there are a couple of witnesses. I try hard not to show anything on my face and even harder not to look at JD. A *couple* of witnesses? Last I heard, there was only one.

The cop says that they have reason to believe that whoever did it was a high school student who probably lives in the area. He nods to the vice-principal, who flips a switch. The composite of the suspect appears on a screen over their heads. I relax a little. It still doesn't look like me. It looks even less like JD.

The cop tells us that if any of us know anything, anything at all, we should tell the police. He says maybe we've heard something. Or maybe we've noticed a friend or an acquaintance is acting differently. He says it's hard to hide something like killing someone. He says he knows there are people who know something, and all he wants is for those people to come forward. He says it's the least we could do for a man like Mr. Braithwaite, who spent his life giving so much to the community, who started off from such humble beginnings and who accomplished so much. He thanks us for our time and we are dismissed. JD and I split up. We have different classes—he has math, which I've already had. I have geography.

JD is waiting for me in the hall after class. We head for the main doors. As we pass the office, we see the same homicide cop. He's talking to the vice-principal. The vice-principal hands him a book. JD and I both see what it is. It's a yearbook. I start to get a bad feeling. Maybe the cop is going to show the yearbook to his witnesses. Maybe the witnesses will pick me out. Me, not JD.

I wait until we are far from the school and there is no one around us. Then I say to JD, "What are we going to do?"

"We're not going to do anything," JD says.

"But you killed that guy," I say. I think it's the first time I've said it out loud. "And they have witnesses."

"You heard what he said," JD says. "You saw the sketch. They're still only looking for one person, Q, which means that their witnesses can't be any good."

"Maybe he didn't tell us everything," I say. "Cops are like that. They always keep certain information from the public. That way they can trip up the bad guys." The bad guys—JD and me.

"You're driving me crazy, you know that?" JD says. "You keep panicking when I tell you to stay calm. Do you see me panicking? No. *I'm* staying calm, even though none of this would have happened if it wasn't for you."

"What?" I stare at him. What is he talking about? "I didn't shoot the guy."

"You stole that stuff. Do you know what would have happened if I'd been arrested for stealing from that truck? Do you have any idea what my father would have done to me if I'd been arrested? Do you?" His face is all red and he's angry, but he's talking in a raspy whisper so no one but me can hear him, even though there's no one but me around.

"You shot a guy," I said. "What do you think he's going to do if he finds out about that?"

"He's not going to find out."

"Geez, why did you even do it?" I say. "Why did you even have a gun on you?"

He gives me a kind of blank look. Then he shakes his head. "If you ask me, all that hero stuff that they said about that guy, I bet most of it isn't even true."

"That doesn't matter," I say. "What matters is he's dead and the cops are doing everything they can to find who did it."

Chapter Nine

I don't sleep well that night. I wake up the next morning feeling like I've pulled back-to-back all-nighters. JD comes to pick me up again. Before, it was always the other way around. Before, he always expected me to go to his house and pick him up. Now it's like he wants to make sure he knows where I am and what I'm doing. He's nervous, I realize, and that makes me nervous.

We get to school. The first thing we see is Detective Tanner and another plainclothes cop, probably another homicide detective. They are in the office. This time they're talking to the principal.

An announcement comes over the PA system while we're in homeroom. The police are going to be talking to students today. They just want to ask some questions. No one is obligated to speak to them. If you get called down to the office to speak to the police, but you don't want to speak to them, you just have to say so. It's your right. But the principal says he hopes everyone will cooperate because the police are just doing their job. I wonder who the police want to speak to. I wonder if I'll be called to the office. I wonder what will happen if I say I don't want to speak to them.

First class of the day: Nothing happens.

Second class of the day: Someone says that the police are asking to talk to boys with sandy-colored hair. Halfway through class, Jonathan Randall, who has sandy-colored hair, is asked to go to the office.

When he comes back fifteen minutes later, he whispers to the kid sitting behind me, "They wanted to know where I was on Sunday afternoon when that guy got killed."

"Where were you?" the kid next to him says.

"I was at my grandmother's house, helping her clean up her yard. My mother was there too."

Where was I Sunday afternoon? If they call me, what will I say?

Lunch: JD is waiting for me at my locker. He drags me into an empty classroom and shuts the door.

"Did they call you yet?" he says.

I shake my head.

"What are you going to tell them?" he says.

"I'll say we were together," I tell him. "We can back each other up."

JD is shaking his head before I finish speaking. "It's better if you don't mention my name."

I think, Better for who?

"So what should I tell them?"

Before JD can answer, the vice-principal opens the classroom door.

"You boys know you shouldn't be in here," he says to both of us. He looks at me. "Quentin, the police want to speak with you. Please report to the office."

He stands there, holding the door open for us to leave, so I can't talk to JD. He sticks with me all the way down to the office. Inside, there are two other guys sitting on a bench, waiting. They both have sandy-colored hair. I take a place on the bench beside them.

One by one they get called in by Detective Tanner. While the second one is inside, another couple of guys with sandy-colored hair join me on the bench. I hear the vice-principal say, "I think that's everyone."

Then it's my turn. I feel myself trembling all over, but I hope it doesn't show. I still haven't decided what to say.

Chapter Ten

Detective Tanner introduces me to his partner, who is sitting behind a desk. On the desk is a yearbook, a piece of paper with a list of names on it and a notebook. Detective Tanner tells me to take a seat. He asks my name and if I like school. I say, "It's okay." He asks me what my favorite subject is. I say I don't really have one. He asks if I play any sports. I tell him I'm not on any teams, but that, yeah, I play a little football in the park sometimes, with some guys I know. I also play a little road hockey.

Then he says, "Do you know what we want to talk to you about today, Quentin?"

I say, "I heard it was about that man who was killed."

Detective Tanner nods. He says, "You don't have to answer any questions if you don't want to, Quentin. I want to make it clear that we do not consider you a suspect at this time."

At this time.

"But if you agree to answer our questions, Quentin, anything you tell us can be used against you as evidence in a court or other proceeding. Do you understand?"

I nod.

"You also have the right to have a parent here with you. Do you want a parent here?"

I say, "No."

He asks if I want anyone else here with me. I say, "No."

He says, "Do you want to answer our questions?"

I say, "Sure." The whole time that he's talking and I'm answering, I'm trying to think of what I'm going to tell them.

He says, "Can you let us know where you were at three o'clock on Sunday afternoon, Quentin?"

I say, "I was down at the beach with a friend of mine." I don't say it because I want to get JD into trouble. I say it because it's more or less true. I say it because they're looking for one guy and I was with someone else. They can ask that person. I say I was at the beach because I *was* at the beach. Maybe I wasn't there at three o'clock, but I was there earlier. Maybe someone will remember seeing me there. I'm pretty sure no one will remember when I left. There were a whole lot of people at the beach that day.

He asks me when I left the beach. I think a minute, like I'm trying to remember. If I was at the beach at three, that means I was at least a half hour away from where I really was. I decide not to make things too complicated. I say, "I'm not really sure. It must have been around then, around three o'clock. We went back to my friend's house."

He asks me if I knew Richard Braithwaite, the man who was killed.

I say, "No."

He asks me the name of the friend I was with. I tell him. He asks me if JD goes to this school. I say, "Yes."

He says, "Thank you, Quentin. You can go now."

And that's it.

I get up and leave. I feel sick inside. I think, Maybe I should just tell them the truth. But I'm too scared. I was stealing from the guy when he was shot. If they find out what I did, even though I wasn't the one who pulled the trigger, I will be in big trouble. And there's still a good chance they won't find out I was there.

I'm surprised that JD isn't waiting for me after school. I don't find out why until later, when I'm at home eating some microwave pizza while my mother is at work. I hear someone knocking on the door. I freeze up because I think it might be the police. It isn't. It's JD, his backpack over his shoulder, a mad look on his face. As soon as I open the door, he pushes his way inside. He says, "I told you not to mention my name." He's mad.

I explain to him why I did it. I say, "In case they want to talk to you, we can back each other up."

He says, "In case? They called me down to the office, Q."

"Okay," I say slowly. "And you backed me up, right?"

He gives me a sharp look. "When people back each other up, they usually know what each other is going to say," he says. "And when the cops talk to you, they don't tell you what anyone else said."

Oh.

"They asked me where I was at three o'clock on Sunday afternoon," he says.

I'm standing there on the carpet inside the door, but I feel like I'm not really there. JD is right. If he was going to back me up, first he'd have to know what I said to the cops. And he didn't know. He still doesn't. That means I could be in big trouble. I look at JD.

"What did you tell them?" I say.

"I don't look anything like the description they put out," he says. "So I figured the only reason they wanted to talk to me was because you said something. That pissed me off, Q. I didn't know what you might have told them. I didn't know if you fell apart in there or if you managed to stay calm."

I start to feel sick all over again. "What did you tell them, JD?"

"I said I was with you."

That surprises me. "Did they want to know where we were?"

JD nods.

"And?"

"I said we were at the beach," JD says. "I said I wasn't sure exactly when we left. Maybe three fifteen or three thirty. I figured that was safe. It was about four o'clock when Leah walked in on us. We could have ridden back to my house by then, right?"

I want to hug him. So far we're okay.

He says, "You got any more pizza? I haven't eaten yet."

"I can nuke some for you," I say.

He says, "Great. I have to use the bathroom."

He's back a few minutes later. He eats his pizza. We talk about what to do if the cops want to talk to either one of us again. Then he leaves. Afterward, even though we are in the clear so far, I think again that maybe I should just go to the cops and tell them what happened. Mostly, I want it to be over with. I want the whole thing to go away.

It doesn't.

Chapter Eleven

For once, JD does not pick me up for school. I don't even see him for the first part of the day. But that isn't unusual. He's only in one of my classes.

When I finally do see him, he's quiet. Serious. He tells me he has to go right home after school. He tells me his father has been giving him a hard time about his homework habits.

That night, after supper, someone knocks on the apartment door. My mother, who has the night off, answers. I hear a male voice. I hear the word "police." I hear the words "search warrant." I hear my mother say, "I don't understand." Then the living room is crowded with people.

There are two cops in plain clothes. One of them is the homicide cop who was at my school earlier. There are also four uniformed police officers. The homicide cop from my school, Detective Brian Tanner, is showing my mother the search warrant. When he sees me, he asks me for my name. I tell him. My mother says again, "I don't understand." She looks at me like she's waiting for me to explain.

One of the uniformed police officers stands inside the door to our apartment. I get the feeling that's so I won't try to run away. Everyone else puts on plastic gloves. Detective Tanner asks my mother where my bedroom is. He also asks where she keeps the laundry hamper. She still has a stunned look on her face as she answers. Then off they go to look. Because he asked about the laundry hamper, I guess they are looking for my clothes. Boy, am I ever glad that JD burned them and then buried them.

From down the hall where my bedroom is, I hear one cop call to Detective Tanner. A minute later, he's back in the living room holding up a shirt and a pair of jeans. My shirt. My jeans. The same ones I was wearing on Sunday when JD shot that guy. There's blood all over the shirt. I don't get it. JD put everything in the washing machine. Did he forget to put in detergent? Why do my clothes look like they were never washed? And—biggest question of all—how did they get in my room?

The next thing I know, Detective Tanner is telling me that I am under arrest for the murder of Richard Braithwaite. I am handcuffed. My mother stands there, stunned. Her mouth hangs open a little as she listens to Detective Tanner tell me about my rights. I'm listening. I hear words. But nothing sticks in my head. Nothing except that one question: How did those clothes get into the apartment?

They take me downtown. They tell me my rights and they make me sign a piece of paper that says I understand. They ask me if I want my mother in the room. I say no. They ask me if I want a lawyer or another adult. I say no. They tell me they're going to videotape the interview. They ask me why I lied to them. They say I should tell them now exactly what happened. I tell them. I say, "I stole from the guy, but JD shot him."

They just look at me.

"It's true," I say. "JD is the one who shot him."

Finally Detective Tanner says, "Someone saw you in the park the day before Richard Braithwaite was shot. That person says you were arguing with Mr. Braithwaite. That person saw you make a gesture with your hand, as if you were shooting him."

I try to remember, and then I do. JD wasn't around when that happened. He was behind the building where the change rooms are.

"Someone saw you go into the alley where Mr. Braithwaite was shot," he says. "Just you."

"But JD was there."

"JD says he was at home when it happened," Detective Tanner says. "He says you were at the beach together earlier in the day, but then you split up. He says you came to his house around a quarter to four and told him you shot someone. He says you begged him to help you and that he lent you some clothes so that you could get home. He says he also helped you wash off your bicycle and that you left with your clothes in a bag. He says you threatened to harm him if he didn't keep quiet. But he finally decided to come forward."

"That's not true," I say. "He was there. Did you look for his clothes? Did you check them out?"

"He gave us the clothes he was wearing that day," he says.

JD lied to me about washing our clothes and then burning them. He washed his. He probably got everything out. It was his word against mine now, and my clothes had blood all over them.

They don't let me go home. Instead, I go to court and then I get transferred to a detention facility.

My mother comes to see me. I tell her the truth. All of it. I'm ashamed of myself, and I feel bad telling her I stole from the man who got shot. But I tell her I didn't shoot him. She says she believes me, but she's crying when she says it.

She cries the next day too, when she comes to see me again. She cries when she tells me what people in our building are saying about me and about her. I tell her, Don't listen. I tell her, It's not your fault. I tell her, I didn't shoot that man.

Before she leaves, she hands me an envelope that she says JD's sister gave her to give to me. I open it. Inside there is a photograph—this time it's a picture of Leah and me. I didn't notice it when JD was taking the picture, but I see it now. Leah's head is turned just a little toward me and she's smiling. She's smiling *at me*.

In the bottom right-hand corner of the picture, put there automatically by the camera, is the time and the date. I stare at it and wish the day that Leah smiled at me like that wasn't also the day that man died.

"She said to tell you that she believes in you no matter what," my mother says. "She also said to tell you that JD feels terrible about going to the police, but that he had to do it."

I stare at the picture. I wish I was in it, standing next to Leah. I wish I could stand next to her forever.

Chapter Twelve

After my mother leaves, I take the picture back to my room and tuck it into a book that they let me borrow from the bookshelf they call the library. Also inside the book is the picture of JD and me that Leah took. There I am in the denim shirt and jeans that the police have, only in the picture they aren't splattered with blood. And there's JD in the clothes he was wearing that day, also looking nice and clean. I think about what Leah told my mother, and I know it's not true. JD doesn't feel terrible. He feels relieved. Relieved that I am the one who is locked up and he is the one who is the good citizen. I want to rip up the picture, but I don't. Instead, I stare at JD standing there beside his bike, smiling for Leah's camera. In the picture, he knows he has a gun stuck in the back of his pants, but I don't. In the picture, I'm also smiling at Leah, but for a different reason than JD.

The next afternoon, I am sitting in a big room where there is a TV, a couple of tables, and some chairs and couches. Guys are watching TV. Guys are playing cards. Guys are just talking. I am sitting in the corner with my library book. To people who don't look closely, it would seem as if I'm reading. But really I'm looking at the picture of Leah and me. I close the book fast when one of the guards comes over to me.

"Quentin, the police are here to see you," he says.

Finally. I called Detective Tanner first thing in the morning, but all I got was his voice mail. I left a message.

I stand up, holding the book. I don't want to leave it in the room where anyone can take it, but I'm not sure if I'm allowed to bring it with me.

"Come on," the guard says. So I follow him, carrying the book.

Detective Tanner is in an office, waiting for me. He tells me to sit down.

I sit.

He sits down too. He says, "What did you want to talk to me about, Quentin?"

"I wanted to tell you that I didn't do it."

He looks at me. "The man's blood is all over your clothes, Quentin."

"That's because I was standing right next to him when JD shot him. I'm lucky he didn't shoot me instead."

"There's nothing on JD's clothes. They're clean."

"That's because he washed his clothes. We went to his house right after it happened and we took off our clothes. JD sent me upstairs to get clean clothes. He said he was going to put our clothes in the washing machine, but he must have only washed his own clothes."

Detective Tanner does not look impressed.

"He was with me," I insist. "I took stuff from the guy's truck. He caught me and was going to call the cops. That's when JD shot him. I was going to tell you. But JD went to you first. He knows you were only looking for one guy. But he was there."

"You're not telling me anything that you haven't already told me, Quentin." Detective Tanner stood up. "You should do yourself a favor. Tell the truth. And tell us where the gun is. If there's one thing we don't need in this city, it's another gun out there waiting for some other kid to use it."

I get up too. "Wait," I say. I forget that I have a book in my lap, and it falls to the floor. The pictures fall out and slide across the floor to where Detective Tanner is standing. He bends to pick them up. He glances at them, and then he starts to hand them back to me. Then he looks at them again and frowns.

He says, "Tell me again what you and JD did that day. Start at the beginning."

So I tell him I went to JD's house.

"What time?" he says.

I tell him. I say we got our bikes out and we rode a few blocks away to smoke up.

"Before you did that, what did you do?" he says.

"Before?"

"Before you left JD's house."

"We didn't do anything. Leah took our picture and then we left."

"This picture?" he says, holding it up.

"Yeah." I tell him again everything we did that day—my version. The true version.

"Did JD change before he left the house?"

"Change?"

"Change his clothes. Before you left his house, after this picture was taken, did he change his clothes?"

I'm really confused now. "No," I say.

"What about later? Did he change his clothes later?"

"Sure," I say. "We both did. After we got back to his house, we took off our clothes and put on clean clothes." I tell him what I put on and what JD put on.

"I'm going to need this picture," he says. He hands me back the other one, the one of Leah and me.

"What's the matter?" I say.

But he doesn't tell me. Not right away, anyway.

Chapter Thirteen

I'm surprised when they let me see JD. I am also surprised that he smiles at me when I come through the door. I go over to the table where he's sitting, and I sit down opposite him. I get another surprise when he says, "How's Leah?"

"You don't know?" I say. "She's your sister."

"She hasn't come to see me. She won't even talk to me. I don't know if it's because of the guy or because of you."

"It's both," I tell him. I know because Leah told me. But she didn't tell me that she hasn't been to see JD. "She says she can't believe you would carry a gun around. She can't believe you would shoot someone. And she can't believe you'd put all the blame on me." I look at him. "Why did you shoot him, JD?"

He shrugs. "He pissed me off, that's all. And he was going to screw things up for me with his stupid citizen's arrest. I just got mad, that's all. I just thought, no way is he going to screw things up for me." He shakes his head. "You know what I've been thinking, Q? I've been thinking that all those anti-gun nuts are maybe right. If I hadn't had that gun with me, I never would have shot that guy. My sister wouldn't be acting like I have the plague. And I wouldn't be in here while you're out there."

He's right. I am out. Not completely out of trouble, but at least out of detention while I wait to see what happens next. Because what happened was this: When the cops said that JD had voluntarily given them the clothes he was wearing that day, I assumed that was really what he had done.

It wasn't.

He gave them clothes that were similar. He had been wearing black jeans with a belt that had a big square buckle on it and a white T-shirt with a dark blue stripe across the chest. He gave them a different pair of black jeans, and a T-shirt with a *light* blue stripe across the chest. He didn't think anyone who might have seen him would notice the difference.

But Detective Tanner has been a cop for a long time and I guess he is a good one because first he noticed the time and date that Leah's camera had automatically put at the bottom of the photo. And then he noticed that the clothes JD was wearing in the picture weren't the same ones he gave to the police. So he got a search warrant and searched JD's house. He didn't tell JD about the picture Leah had taken, and he didn't find the black jeans, or the shirt with the dark blue stripe that JD was wearing in that picture.

So he came back and talked to me again. I told him that JD said he had burned our clothes and buried them. I told him all the places I could think of where JD might have buried them.

Detective Tanner asked JD to come in for questioning. JD showed up with his father and a lawyer. Detective Tanner had a big paper bag on the table. He opened the bag and pulled out a gun. He said, "You recognize it, JD?"

"I couldn't believe it," JD says to me now in the visiting room. "How did he even know where to look?"

"He asked me if there were places you liked to go, maybe on your bike," I say. "I told him you like riding in the ravines."

JD shakes his head. "I should never have told you I got rid of my clothes. But back then I thought we were going to be okay."

"You said you got rid of *our* clothes," I say. I don't add, *But you lied.*

"It turns out that they couldn't find anything on what was left of the clothes that they could use to say I shot the guy," JD says. "I burned them pretty good. But I had to get rid of the gun, right? So I buried it with the clothes. I didn't think they would ever find it. Turns out that made it even easier for them because they went out with a metal detector. And it turns out that because I was so close to the guy when I shot him, there was some of his blood inside the gun. My lawyer says it's called blowback. And they also got a partial fingerprint off the gun. Mine. And it's good enough that the court will let them say it's a match. My lawyer advised me to cooperate. What could I do? They had me."

He pauses and looks at me. "I told them you had nothing to do with the shooting."

"You did?" I say.

"It's the truth," he says. "I guess you're pretty mad at me, huh?"

I shrug. "I was. But not anymore. It was my own fault I was there. It was my idea to take that stuff."

"Yeah," JD says. We talk a few minutes more. When I get up to leave, he says, "Tell Leah to come and see me sometime, okay? Tell her I miss her."

I promise to do that. And even though I know she's mad at him, I also know that she'll eventually come. She'll have to. He's her brother. They're twins. She loves him.

Norah McClintock is the author of *Tell* and *Snitch*, both Orca Soundings novels. Norah lives in Toronto, Ontario.

Titles in the
Orca Soundings series

Titles in the
Orca Soundings series

Titles in the
Orca Soundings series

Visit www.orcabook.com for more information.

Check out these Orca Currents titles

Check out these Orca Currents titles

Mirror Image

K.L. Denman

Pigboy

Vicki Grant

Queen of the Toilet Bowl

Frieda Wishinsky

See No Evil

Diane Young

Sewer Rats

Sigmund Brouwer

Spoiled Rotten

Dayle Campbell Gaetz

Sudden Impact

Lesley Choyce

Swiped

Michele Martin Bossley

Wired

Sigmund Brouwer

Visit www.orcabook.com for more information.

Quick Picks and Popular Paperbacks nominees
—American Library Association

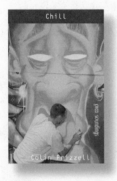

Chill
Colin Frizzell
978-1-55143-507-7 PB
978-1-55143-670-8 HC
AGES 12+ RL 3.5

Battle of the Bands
K.L. Denman
978-1-55143-540-4 PB
978-1-55143-674-6 HC
AGES 12+ RL 2.9

Quick Picks and Popular Paperbacks nominees
—American Library Association

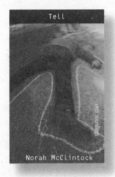

Tell
Norah McClintock
978-1-55143-511-4 PB
978-1-55143-672-2 HC
AGES 12+ RL 4.0

Crush
Carrie Mac
978-1-55143-526-8 PB
978-1-55143-521-3 HC
AGES 12+ RL 3.4

Thunderbowl
Lesley Choyce
978-1-55143-277-9 PB
978-1-55143-552-7 HC
AGES 12+ RL 4.0